THIS WALKER BOOK
BELONGS TO:

....

....

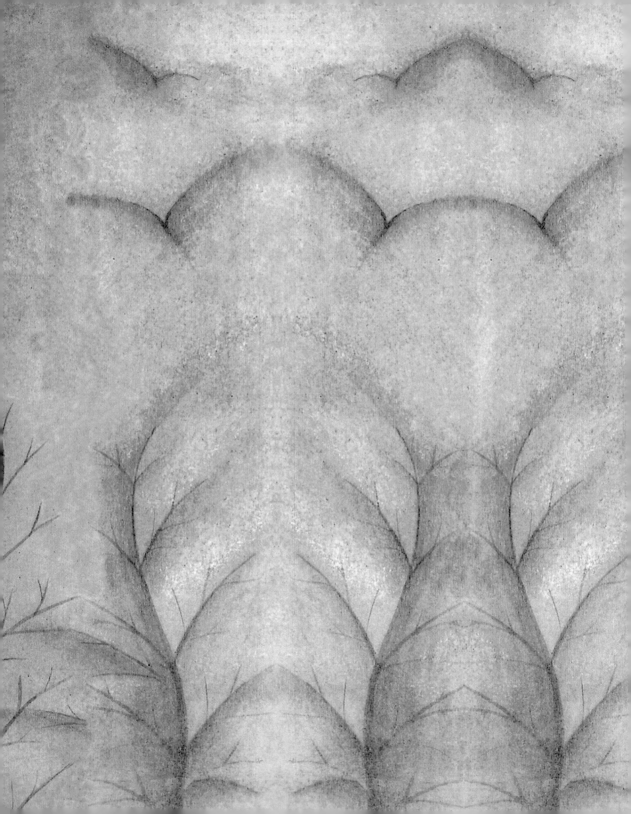

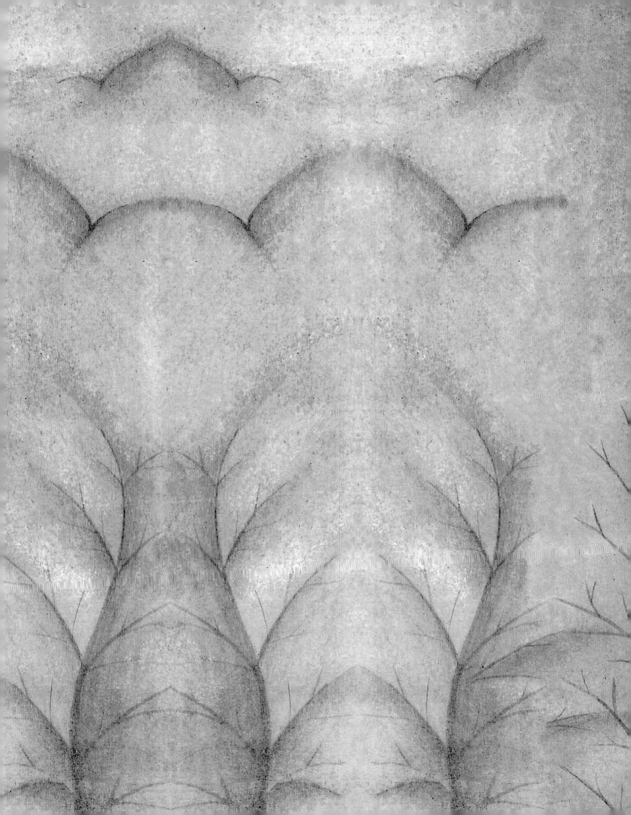

First published in *Fairy Tales* 2000 by Walker Books Ltd
87 Vauxhall Walk, London SE11 5HJ

This edition published 2010

2 4 6 8 10 9 7 5 3 1

This book has been typeset in Palatino

Printed in China

British Library Cataloguing in Publication Data:
a catalogue record for this book is available from the British Library

ISBN 978-1-4063-2979-7

www.walker.co.uk

Rapunzel

BERLIE DOHERTY

Illustrated by

JANE RAY

WALKER BOOKS

AND SUBSIDIARIES

LONDON • BOSTON • SYDNEY

Long, long ago a man and wife lived in a cottage that overlooked a garden belonging to a witch. They would sit at their open window at the end of the day and breathe in all the perfumes of the flowers, and gaze at the misty colours, and say how lucky they were to live there.

"If only we had a child," they said, "there would be nothing left in the world to wish for."

Now, one summer day the wife saw something in the witch's garden that took her breath away. It was a drift of blue rapunzel flowers. "I must have some," she said to her husband. "Please, please, I must have some rapunzel to eat. Fetch me some, fetch me some or I might die. Please, please, husband, fetch me some rapunzel."

The husband was puzzled. "Are you mad?" he said. "I'd have to climb into the witch's garden to get it!"

But it seemed that his wife *was*

mad with longing for the rapunzel flower. "Please, please," she begged him, "get me that rapunzel or I'll die," and at last he gave in to her. When night came he scaled the wall like a cat, plucked a handful of rapunzel and was back over the wall in less time than it takes an owl to blink. His wife made a salad of it and ate it at once.

"Was that good?" Her husband smiled.

"Yes," she said. "More please. I'd like some more. I must have some more. Please, please!" And she begged and pleaded for three whole days till he knew they would both go mad unless he fetched her some.

So when night came he scaled the wall again, quick as a mouse, and was just stooping down with his hands around a bright bunch of the plant when a shadow fell across him.

"What are you doing in my garden?"

The man froze as if he had been turned to stone. There was the witch watching him, and her eyes were as green and deep as bog-ponds.

"I was taking some rapunzel for my sick wife," he said. He was afraid for his life, yet there was no point in pretending anything else; he still had the flowers clutched in his fist.

And besides, the witch could read his secret thoughts.

"Your wife is not sick," smiled the witch. "She longs for rapunzel because of the child she is bearing."

"What?" said the man, and his heart soared with joy.

"Of course you must take her some. Take as much as you want."

"Thank you, thank you." The man fell on his knees in gratitude.

But the witch's smile had turned to frost. "And when your daughter is born, give her to me. I will be her mother."

The man could hear his wife's voice, begging him to bring her the flowers at once. Frightened out of his wits, bewildered and excited all at once, he promised to do as the witch said. Then he gathered up as much rapunzel as he could and climbed the wall to his own small yard.

And, just as the witch had told him, a daughter was born to the man and his wife on the first day of spring. They could think of only one name for her,

and that was Rapunzel. She hardly had time to open her eyes and gaze round at the world before the witch was at their door.

"What do you want?" said the man and his wife, with fear in their hearts.

"My child," said the witch. "I told you. I'm her mother now."

They never saw Rapunzel again. The witch loved her so much that she kept her all to herself. She wouldn't even let her play in the garden in case the man and woman watched her from their window and tried to take her back.

By the time Rapunzel was twelve years old she was so beautiful that the witch could hardly take her eyes off her. "Look at your hair!" she marvelled. "It's like a river of gold, the way it tumbles down your back. I've never seen anything like it." She fingered her own crackly hair and

sighed, and then brushed Rapunzel's until it shone like the sun.

But the witch was worried in case anybody saw Rapunzel and wanted her for themselves. She didn't want to share her with anybody. So she put her in a tower and sealed up the door behind her, and at the end of every day she brought food for her. There was no way into the tower now of course, so what happened was this: the witch would call out,

"Rapunzel, Rapunzel,
let down your hair."

Then Rapunzel would lean out of

her window at the top of the tower and wind her hair round two hooks and lower it, and down it would flow, down and down like a shimmering golden waterfall all the way to the ground. The witch would tuck up her skirts and shin up Rapunzel's hair as if it was a ladder, and when she wanted to go home to bed she would swing back down again.

There wasn't much for Rapunzel to do, shut up there in her high tower, except to dream and sing. She had a lovely voice, and one day a young prince was riding through the forest and he heard her voice and fell in love with it. He had to know who it belonged to. He found the tower but there was no door to it. He walked round and round, looking up hopelessly at its high, smooth walls. Nobody could be in there, surely, he thought, and yet there was the voice, as sweet as a skylark. He was just about to ride away, sure now that he must be imagining it, when he saw the witch coming through the forest towards the tower, and he hid among the bushes.

"Rapunzel, Rapunzel,
let down your hair,"

he heard her say. The singing stopped

and down came the curtain of glorious hair, and up the witch climbed. Now he had no doubt that somebody was hidden in the tower, and he couldn't wait to see who it was.

As soon as the witch had climbed down again and disappeared into the forest, the prince approached the tower. It was almost night by now, and he was a little afraid that he might be under a spell of some sort, he had such longing to see who was sealed in the tower.

"Rapunzel, Rapunzel,
 let down your hair,"

he called, and sure enough the shower of hair came flowing down. The prince swung himself up. Imagine his surprise when he found himself facing a young girl who was so beautiful in the moonlight that she stole his heart away. And imagine her surprise, when she was expecting a green-eyed spiky witch, to see a young man smiling at her.

Rapunzel had never seen a man before. She had no idea what a prince was. She had never heard of love. But she was very happy. The prince stayed with her until a dawn like pearls was creeping across the sky, and when he left her she knew that she couldn't live without him.

He came the next night, and the next, and the next, and when he asked her if she would be his wife she said *yes*, even though she had no idea what a wife was.

"But this is no good, you know," he said. "I have a fine palace just over the hill. That's where we should be."

So they thought up a wonderful plan for Rapunzel's escape. Every time the prince came to see her he brought her some silk, and all day long when she was without him she wove a ladder for herself. It gave her something to do while she was singing, and each rung she wove brought her a step nearer to freedom.

And all would have been well if she hadn't forgotten herself completely one day. This is what happened. The witch climbed up at dusk, as usual, and Rapunzel said carelessly, "I always know when it's you coming. You're so much heavier than..." She went pale and put her hand to her mouth, but the witch slapped it away, quick as a fly.

"Heavier than what? Heavier than who?"

"Than the prince who comes to see me," Rapunzel confessed.

"You wicked girl! You've deceived me!" In a rage that was as wild as a thunderstorm the witch pulled back Rapunzel's wonderful hair and cut it off – snip! She forced her down the silk ladder that would have taken her into the prince's arms, and sent her out into the wilderness to live or to die, she no longer cared which.

That night the prince came to take Rapunzel home with him.

"Rapunzel, Rapunzel,
let down your hair,"

he called, and this time the silk ladder came down. Up he climbed, but when he reached the tower it was not Rapunzel's eyes that he looked into, but the deep bog-pond green of the witch's.

"Ha! Your bird has flown away!" she cackled. "So fly after her!" She cut the silk ladder – snip! and down he tumbled, down and down, and would have broken his neck if he hadn't been saved by a briar bush. But the thorns pierced his eyes and blinded him, and with the witch's laughter ringing in his ears the prince wandered away into a darkness that was deeper than night itself.

He wandered for many days and many weeks and many months, eating nuts and berries that he found on the wayside, and a year and a

day later he came into the same part of the wilderness as Rapunzel. She recognized him at once and ran to him and put her arms round him, and her tears washed his eyes and he could see again.

He took her home to his palace, and they announced their wedding, and the prince and his Rapunzel lived happily ever after.

And as for the witch – well, as far as I know, she's still trapped in the tower.

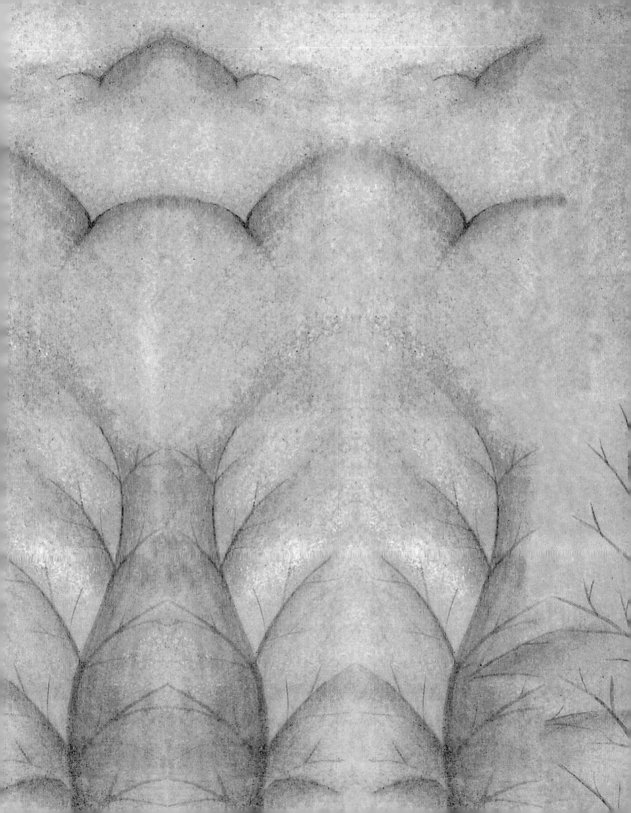

TITLES IN THE FAIRY TALE SERIES

Available from all good bookstores

www.walker.co.uk

FOR THE BEST CHILDREN'S BOOKS, LOOK FOR THE BEAR.